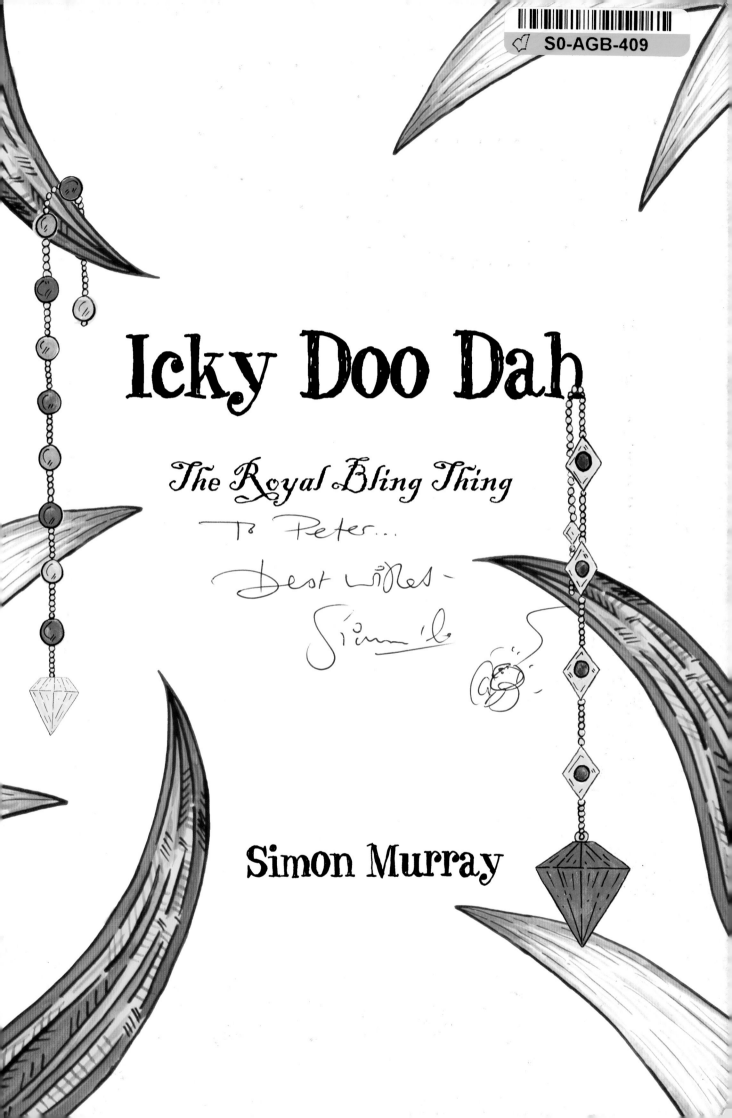

Icky Doo Dah

The Royal Bling Thing

To Peter...

Best wishes -

Simon M.

Simon Murray

For Brian and Pamela

First published in 2007 by SMI Ltd
6 Stanley Road, Newbury, Berkshire, RG14 7PB
Second Edition published 2010

www.ickydoodah.com

ISBN 978-0-9555811-1-3

With great thanks to Martin Maynard, Nikola Hulme, Matthew Murray, Rachel Huggett and Laura Harper.

Congratulations to competition winner Joe Humphrey, aged 7 from Berkshire
who designed an ickydoodastic flag which features in this story!

A CIP catalogue record for this book is available from the British Library.
Printed in Dubai by Oriental Press.

Oh no! Not another

~~A~~ note from the author:

Icky '

~~I~~ would like to thank ~~everyone~~ once
himself

again for ~~their~~ support
his

in creating ~~this~~ new adventure!
his

Simon Murray, August 2007

As another dawn breaks over the middle of Nowhere, I'm getting ready to spend the day all by myself on Copperpot Farm. Again.

Can you spot me in the picture?

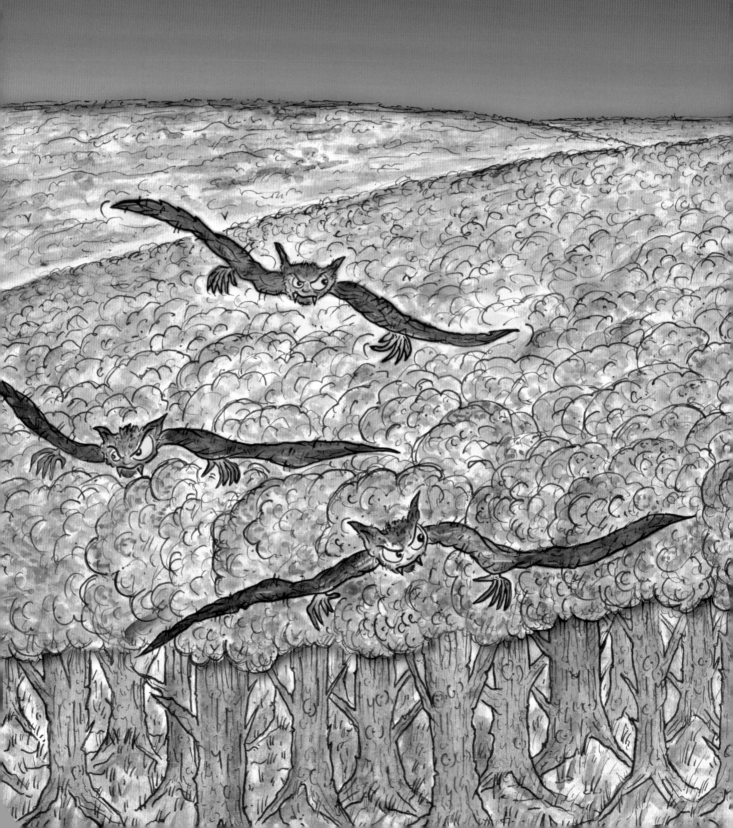

I'm not on the ground
or high in the sky,
I'm not in the trees
or in the clouds way up high!   I'm stuck in the attic -
all dusty and rotten,
stood by the window...

...feeling bored and **forgotten!** I really need to start getting **out** more and **sniffing** out some **serious** mischief. An **icky doo dah** can only **eat** so many spiders on its **own.**

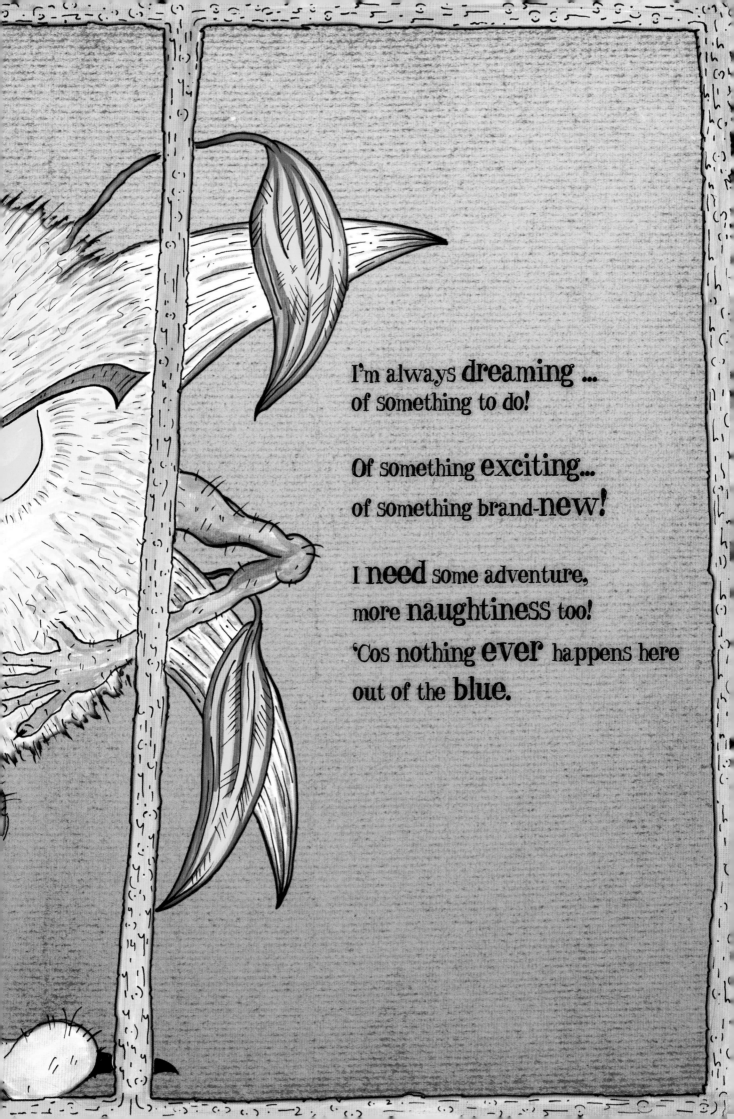

I'm always **dreaming** ...
of something to do!

Of something **exciting**...
of something brand-**new**!

I **need** some adventure,
more **naughtiness** too!
'Cos nothing **ever** happens here
out of the **blue**.

With a flash of **lightning** and a rumble of **thunder...** my **radio** speaks of treasure and **plunder!**

I can see myself now... **jewelled** up to my greedy little **eyes!**
Getting my **mitts** on the bling could be **tricky,** but with a
cracking good plan I **shall** be King Icky!

Crowns of platinum...
...diamonds and gold!
I'll **drop** down from this **attic** and **let** the **story** unfold!

I'll just check the **coast** is clear and that Old Wiff and his **pets** aren't roaming about, before I sneak down from my naughty-nest. I'll snaffle one of these **spiders** on the way **down**.

6, 7, 8, 9, 10...
let's have a
doo dah hoo hah
again!

Now let me see...I'll have a little rumble-rummage through these tatty toy boxes for some tools to help me escape from Copperpot Farm!

With a crash-bang-wallop
and an icky-dicky toot,
I'm off to claim the Crown
and have a doo dah hoot!

I think I'll sniggle-snuggle my way into the **Palace** down that old **chimney**.

Take a deep breath and float on the **breeze**! **Breathe** in tight... 'cos it's **gonna** be a **squeeze**!

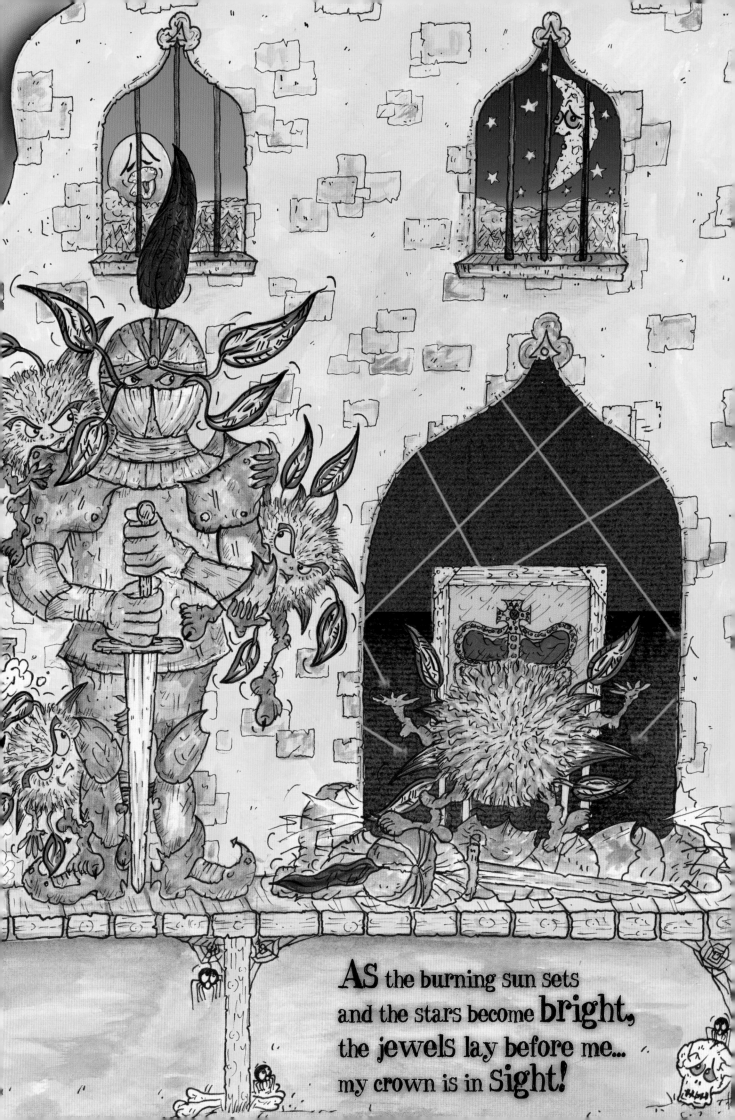

AS the burning sun sets
and the stars become **bright,**
the jewels lay before me...
my crown is in **sight!**

This way... that way... a mischief fest,
when it comes to dodging lasers-
Icky Doo Dah's the best!
My little doo dah claws are sharper than
any diamond – and a million
times rarer!

With a push and a shove,
a smash and a crackle!
I'll grab my royal prize
and have a good old cackle!

Icky's here!

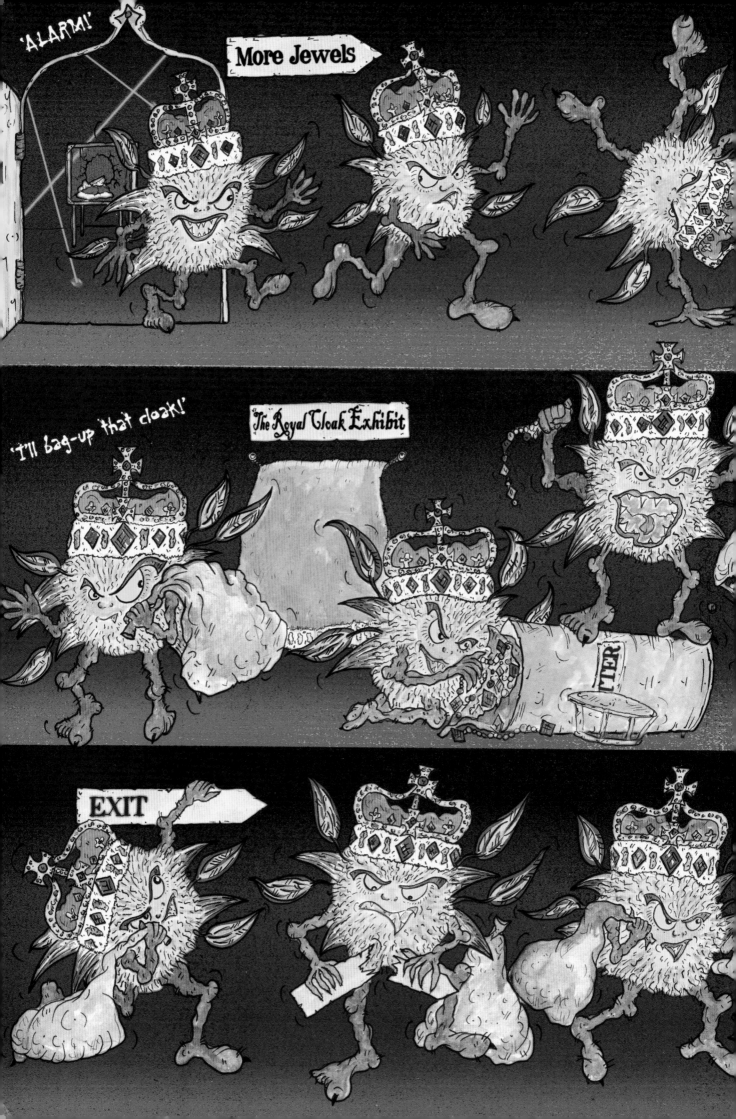

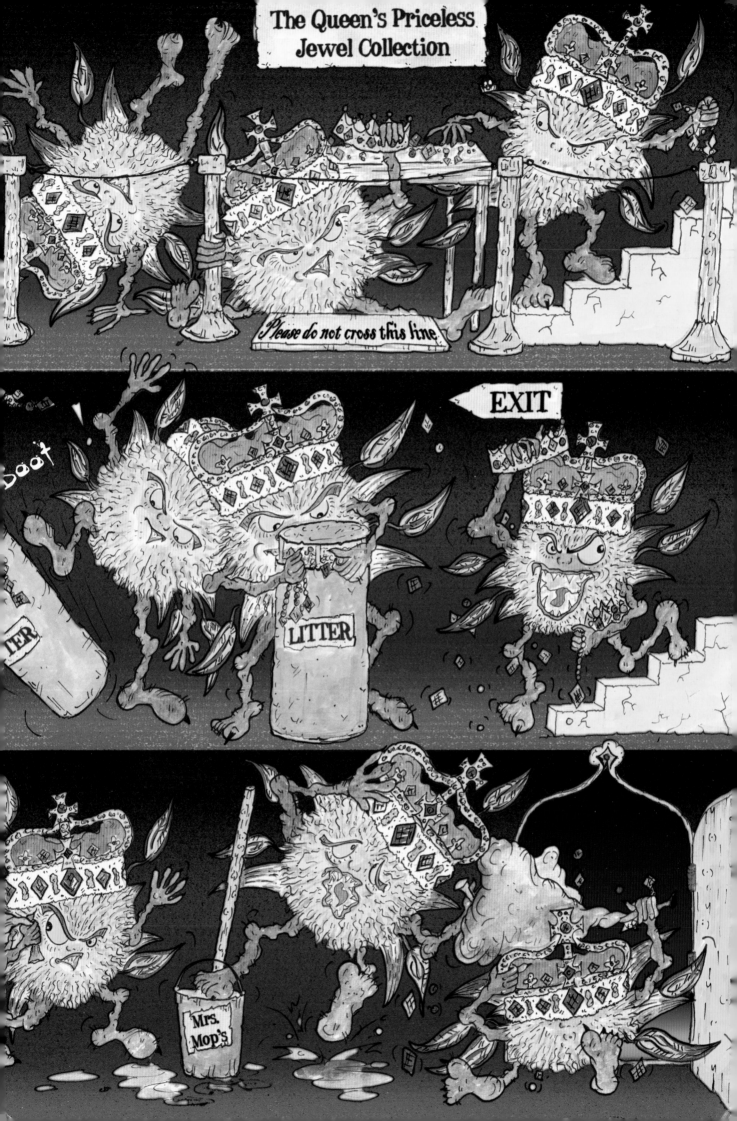

I'm back on my pins!

I've got an **idea** –
I'll escape on a **raven!**
I'll wing it back to the farm
and hide in my **haven!**

But I've got one last **surprise**
tucked up my sleeve...
there's one **thing** to do
before I can **leave!**

I'll throw on my **cloak**
and **lay** down my bag
and from the Queen's Royal Palace
I'll fly Icky's **flag!**

Escaping in style
with a wave of delight-
up to the stars
and still gaining height!

My poor raven's tiring –
with a look of alarm...
but luckily for him
we're near Copperpot Farm!

So as our little bodies plummet
and we begin to crash-land,
I'll be home in a minute
with mischief in hand!

I've arrived back safe
and naughty-
I've got to hide my stash!
I can hear the sirens nearing –
the police will be here in a flash!

Retch and Crackers are
both snoozing,
you think they'd have
more sense!

Plip and Plop just
swim in circles -
they really are quite dense!

Copperpot Farm